AF265864

Copyright © 2024 Juliet Burton
First published in 2024 by Versitality Publishing

Illustrations by Caroline Finlayson
Design and layout and distribution by Spiffing Publishing

ISBN: 978-1-0687446-0-0

The First Christmas Star

by Juliet Burton

Illustrations by Caroline Finlayson

For Mark

with thanks for his encouragement
and choosing this for the carol service

Versitality

PUBLISHING

Can you imagine the enormous surprise
When the scholarly men who studied the skies

Looked up to the heavens one cloudless night
And saw a new star - dazzling and bright

Those three sober men started dancing a jig
Something was up and it had to be...

Then Mary was given a huge surprise too
An angel appeared right out of the blue

His name was Gabriel and what he told Mary
Many young girls would have found very scary

God had chosen her to give birth to His Son
The Everlasting King, the Most...

Holy One

Mary loved Joseph, he was so gentle and kind
But surely he'd think she was out of her mind?

But Joseph just said that she must be dreaming
Or else he thought she was terribly scheming

Then Joseph dreamt she'd still be his wife
And together they'd treasure this special...

new life

Those scholarly men consulted their scrolls
They read of a king - a saviour of souls -

The Christ who was promised through prophets of old
So frankincense and myrrh and gold

Seemed fitting gifts to bring from afar
As they travelled towards that twinkling...

new star

Mary found Elizabeth singing to God
Her husband joining with a reverent nod

His voice had vanished when he doubted God's gift
Which had made Angel Gabriel a little bit miffed!

For **they'd** been promised a surprise baby too -
He'd prepare the way for...

You Know Who!

He'd teach the people about heavenly things
About God's love and the High King of kings.

Then Mary to Bethlehem on a donkey must go
Caesar'd ordered a tax - and they couldn't say "No"

But the town was full with no room at the inn
And her baby's birth was about to...

begin!

The star-gazing kings were still on their way
They'd consulted king Herod who'd made them delay

Now they were hurrying to Bethlehem town
Thrilled that their star was still shining down

Eager to worship the babe whom they sought
And give him the treasures they'd...

carefully
brought

Some shepherds were quietly watching their sheep
Some staying awake, some falling asleep

When an **angel** appeared in a glorious light
He quickly told them not to take fright

He had wonderful news - the birth of a boy
God's very own Son - the cause of...

great joy!

The shepherds, excited hurried off to see
They knew the place where a lamb might be

The angel had said they'd find the babe in a manger
Then more angels came - it couldn't have been stranger

Could this be the Messiah with parents so poor?
The saviour king they had all...

waited for?

The answer was "yes" as soon as they saw him
Though the light in the stable was terribly dim

There was nothing of darkness in that holy place
They fell to their knees as they gazed at his face

And Mary and Joseph smiled at each other
Mary's heart bursting with love as...

his mother

And the star in the sky was smiling too
Beaming in wonder - Oh yes it knew

That this was the MOST exciting night
Because JESUS is our true guiding light

But his birth at Bethlehem was only the start -
For now his love can shine in...

your heart!